Merlin and Guinevere

A Happenstance Meeting

By

R.D. Shanks

Dedicated to Mum and Dad.

Thanks for reading me so many stories.

Cover design by Catherine Redgate.

Contents

Prologue

On the Magical Arts

Few people deny the power of magic. Even fewer understand it.

Magic is an ancient art. Magic called this world home long before the first humans took their first steps, and it will live here long after we are gone.

Years ago, the magical arts were at their strongest. Great and worthy men and women learned of the arts and devoted themselves to the study of magic. Few people have ever passed the tests set by the ancient laws of magic. Those who do pass, however, are capable of using the terrific powers of the elements, of earth, fire, air and water.

Magic, alas, no longer flourishes in our world. Years ago, practitioners of the magical arts understood the careful relationship one must cultivate with nature to earn the gift of magic. In our modern age, this fact has long since been forgotten.

Many people believe that great sorcerers are born with their skill. This is untrue. Men and women must undergo fearsome trials to receive their gifts. Once blessed with magic, practitioners must further develop their art or it will soon leave them in search of a new master. Magic grows bored easily.

Years ago, a small number of sorcerers attained such amazing strength that they could lead others to the source of magical power. Guinevere was one such sorcerer…

Chapter One

The Boy Merlin

Merlin had lived his whole life in the cottage near the harbour with his father. He could hear the crash of the waves when he lay awake at night. Merlin loved to scramble about on the rocks but liked his home far less when the waves crept in far enough to flood the cottage. His father joked sometimes that there were more rainy days than sunrises in Scotia.

That day, the day when everything in Merlin's life began to take a strange turn, his father was out at sea. The villagers depended on the sea for their survival and were fiercely proud of their fishermen. Merlin's father, Murrow, was popular among the villagers. He was loud and broad-shouldered, the kind of man people found it difficult to ignore. Merlin, on the other hand, was quite a different story.

"Why don't you go to the rock pools with the others?" suggested Murrow earlier that morning, "Neil's boy found a crab yesterday."

Merlin smiled and nodded and bid his father goodbye. As usual, he didn't follow his advice.

He was clambering over rocks on the shorefront when Happenstance started to act rather strangely. Murrow often said that Merlin spend too much time alone, but Merlin was never really by himself: Happenstance the cat followed him like a shadow. He had appeared as a kitten at the cottage door out of nowhere, as though he had been ordered to take the boy as his owner. Or perhaps he had just been drawn to the smell of fish.

Merlin made sure to keep a safe distance from the other boys on the rocks. He found it easier when he was the one ignoring them, instead of the other way around. He knew that if he tried to join them they would soon move off without him. It wasn't out of nastiness; it was just quite easy to forget that Merlin was there. He was shy and often far away in thought, and paler than most people in the village.

Merlin was climbing across a rock when Happenstance let out a piercing meow. He turned to see the cat sniffing the air. Happenstance, who was fat, black and fluffy, looked much more alert than usual. Whenever he wasn't following Merlin, he would curl up somewhere dry and sleep, and if he thought Merlin had taken too much exercise, he would simply roll on his back and meow until Merlin carried him home.

"What is it, Happenstance? Do you smell some fish?"

Merlin bent down to stroke the cat's head. Happenstance kept his nose in the air before yowling in excitement. He bounced around and chased his tail. When he noticed the boy laughing, he rolled over on his back and tried to look dignified when Merlin scooped him up.

They passed the group of boys on their way to the cottage. One boy caught sight of Merlin whispering to the cat and smirked nastily, but the others didn't seem to notice him at all.

It was tricky to scramble up the hill to the cottage without carrying a big fat cat, but Merlin had mastered the art. When they reached the top Happenstance let out another meow. Merlin looked back and spotted a strange sight in the harbour. A small ship had appeared; it looked nothing like the fishing boats Merlin was used to watching. Even from a distance he could tell it must have travelled a long way from foreign shores. No craftsmen in Scotia made ships like that. The sail danced in the wind but whoever sailed there lurked out of sight.

He heard shouts behind him. He turned and saw the boys he'd left behind running pell-mell across the rocks towards the harbour. Merlin decided to watch from the seclusion of the cottage window. Happenstance, who hated the wind, especially since he had only recently licked his fur into place, thought this was a great idea.

Chapter Two

The Stranger

Merlin was waiting by the hearth when his father came home, dangling his fishing net across his shoulders. Happenstance had spent the entire afternoon snoozing in front of the fire and only lazily lifted his head to inspect Murrow as he drew closer.

"Did you see the ship, son?" asked Murrow.

The whole village was buzzing with excitement. Even Merlin, who had only glimpsed the furore from afar, was practically bouncing with anticipation.

"I did! Who sailed here? Did they come to the village by accident?"

"That's what we all thought at first," replied Murrow. He cast his net aside and took a seat beside his son. "The ship must have come all the way from the Southern Isles. But we knew it was no accident," here he paused for effect, "When *she* walked into the village."

"She?" blinked Merlin. "Someone from the ship?"

"Oh yes," smiled Murrow. Enjoying the rapt attention of his son, he held Merlin in suspense while he lifted the kettle above the fire to boil.

"Yes?" urged Merlin. Happenstance meowed in his sleep.

"That was no ordinary ship. It is captained by a *sorcerer*."

"What do you mean? A witch?"

"I've heard they call themselves sorcerers. But that's all I know about it. All anyone knows."

"But how did you know about the sorcerer? Did she show you magic?" Merlin's pale eyes were bright with interest.

"No, not that I saw. But you could tell – there was nothing normal about any of it."

"Father, please tell me what happened when the sorcerer came into the village. From the start!"

Murrow laughed. "Alright, then. I wish you took this much interest in fishing! The ship was there for hours before we found its crew. I was in the market with the others when the Lady appeared."

"The Lady-"

"I thought you wanted to hear?" grinned his father. "Yes, the Lady. She walked through the village with a crowd of strange attendants. That's when the whispers began. You see, her attendants were like no creature I've ever seen. It was hard to see exactly, because they were all wearing hoods and cloaks. But I got close enough to look under their hoods…They had blue skin, and it seemed to ripple…" Here he tailed off, distracted by the mystery of the Lady's attendants.

"Father, please!" called Merlin. Happenstance wondered what all the fuss was about.

"Yes, everyone asked questions but the attendants didn't speak a word to anyone. The Lady walked in front. She wore her hair loose and long, and strolled through the market as though she knew exactly where she was going. I asked for her name and she replied 'Lady Guinevere', but she wouldn't say where she was from. She said she was here to meet someone and thanked us from giving her ship space in our harbour. Then old Abe's wife caught sight of the blue faces under those cloaks and started to shout about witches and demons. And the Lady replied, without batting an eye, that she was a sorcerer. She said that no harm would befall us from hosting her, and that she was only passing though."

"So do sorcerers really exist? How do you know that she wasn't a demon?"

"We don't know, that's the honest truth. But stranger things have happened, even here in Scotia."

Merlin stared deep into the fire. His mind was aflame with his father's revelations. What had brought the so-called Lady Guinevere to these obscure shores? Was there really such a thing as magic in this world?

Chapter Three

Happenstance Leads the Way

Merlin and his father had shared a dinner of fish stew and talked for hours about magic. Stories about the practitioners of magic were shared at every marketplace and every hearth in the village that evening. No one, however, had heard of the Lady Guinevere before. Murrow puzzled over the attendants that had followed in Guinevere's wake without saying a word. He had heard from travellers about lands far away where giant beasts stalked men like rabbits but none of them had ever met a sorcerer. Whispers had reached their shores about dark magic wreaking havoc across in Eyrieland. Murrow fell asleep wondering whether they were right to have let Guinevere pass freely through the village. Merlin lay awake listening to the waves crash against the rocks.

Merlin fell asleep after what felt like hours. He only enjoyed a wink of sleep before he woke with a start. In the dark he saw two bright eyes above him. Happenstance meowed and prodded Murrow's nose once more with his paw for good measure.

"Oh, Happenstance…" he mumbled, "Do you want to go outside?"

The cat meowed in agreement. He trotted off towards the door, deftly steering clear of any obstacles in his path. Merlin stumbled towards the door blindly.

Outside the darkness was relieved slightly by the twinkling stars. Merlin could see the outline of Happenstance in front.

"Are you happy now?" he whispered.

He kneeled down to stroke the cat's head. Happenstance meowed again, louder this time.

"It isn't breakfast time yet! Please be quiet, Happenstance. I'm going back to sleep."

As soon as he tried to turn away, Happenstance began to wind between his legs, purring. Once Merlin stopped moving, the cat started to meow while taking slow steps backwards. He purred again when Merlin took a few nervous steps towards him.

"Oh, for goodness…You want me to follow you?"

Happenstance meowed in response. Merlin patted him and let the cat lead the way. Every few steps Happenstance turned to check that the boy was still behind him. Merlin was thankful for the light of the stars; without them he would have tripped and stumbled twice as much. He expected the cat to be leading him towards something fishy, but instead Happenstance led him away from the village.

After a while Happenstance paused to style the fur on his face. Merlin couldn't see the cottage behind them anymore. The darkness seemed to grow more complete as they walked further away from the shore.

"You are a weird cat, Happenstance." said Merlin. He had kept on his day-clothes to guard against the cold but he was still shivering. "At least it's not raining. How far do we have to go? I can't sleep all day like you, you know."

Happenstance meowed and rubbed against the boy's legs. Then he stretched and started to saunter towards the woods.

"I won't be able to see in there…" said Merlin, growing afraid. Had the sorcerer bewitched his cat? Was he walking into a trap?

As soon as this thought entered his head, a ball of light appeared. It floated in the air in front of him. He blinked in surprise. He opened his eyes to find that more lights had appeared, marking out a path through the woods. It looked as though he and Happenstance were expected.

"I hope you know what you're doing..." whispered the boy.

The cat purred in response and rolled onto his back. Merlin smiled and scooped him up. He took a deep breath and, shivering, began to follow the strange lights into the woods.

Chapter Four

In the Woods

Deeper into the woods they walked, following the floating lights. Merlin was nervous but he trusted Happenstance, and the cat was purring quite contentedly in his arms. Soon Merlin noticed that the lights were leading him downhill. Looking down into the small close below, he saw a circle of the lights that had guided him, but even bigger and brighter. He had a clear view of the gathering that waited for him.

Happenstance struggled out of his arms and raced down the slope. The woman seated on a tree stump below welcomed him onto her lap. Merlin felt too apprehensive to take another step. The dozen or so hooded figures that stood around the circle could only be the blue-faced attendants that his father had described. That meant that the woman, who was now smiling up at him, must be the Lady Guinevere.

Merlin at last understood why the villagers had been so suspicious of her. There was definitely something magical about the Lady. She had bright, piercing eyes of shocking blue and her red hair fell in waves around her. Her dress was finer than any Merlin had seen before. Her face was youthful, but she could have been any age.

"Is this the one you wanted me to meet?" Guinevere spoke to the cat in a strange accent.

"Good hooman. Loyal hooman." Although Happenstance's mouth didn't open, the voice clearly came from him.

Merlin was too shocked to join the scene below. The woman patted Happenstance, who leapt from her lap. She rose to her feet; at her full height she was taller even than Merlin's father.

"Merlin. Happenstance here told me all about you." She smiled up at him in a curious sort of way.

"But – how?"

"I have my ways."

Merlin was growing frustrated, faced with so many mysteries at once.

"So, you really are a sorcerer? What do you want with Happenstance? With me?"

"So many questions," said Guinevere, although this seemed to please her. "Come, join us, Merlin. I will answer you."

The boy scrambled down, careful not to stumble against the attendants. He kneeled beside Happenstance and stroked the cat for comfort.

"Yes, I am a sorcerer. You can call me Guinevere. I am here to find an assistant. My knowledge of the magical arts has grown too great to keep all to myself. I asked Happenstance here for his advice. Those who understand cats tend to possess a natural affinity for the magical arts."

"So you asked Happenstance…about me?"

"Yes, I did." She stood patiently still, towering above the kneeling boy.

"I don't know anything about sorcerers or magic…"

"I would be surprised if you did. No sorcerer is born in this world. You have time enough to learn."

"But – why?"

Merlin stood up to face her. He was painfully aware of how small and insubstantial he felt beside her.

"I need an assistant. I have business in this part of the world. If you care to learn, you can help me. I will guide you onto the path."

Merlin wondered whether he was dreaming. As if to prove him wrong, Guinevere beckoned over one of her attendants. She lifted back the hood to show the boy what lay beneath. Merlin saw the ripples his father had described: the creature's skin was blue, and seemed to shift across its body, like a series of waves.

"Every sorcerer is chosen by an element. My affinity is with water. My attendants here are drawn from the sea and they have guided me safely over every ocean I have crossed."

Merlin felt slightly less scared of the attendants now he knew that they came from the sea. He tried to sound brave as he asked, "Are there many sorcerers in the world?"

"There are others. None are exactly like me."

Merlin didn't find that hard to believe. This was the strangest thing that had happened to him in his whole eleven years of life.

"What do you mean, that you have business here?" He had a sudden thought. "Did the king send for you?"

"I serve no king. I serve only my own conscience." She smiled, seeing that this shocked Merlin. "I will show you what business I have in these parts."

She lifted her hands together. When she drew them apart, a clear ball of light appeared between them. It grew larger and larger, until Merlin could see shapes moving within it.

"Look closely, Merlin. This will show you exactly what brought me here."

Chapter Five

Events in Eyrieland

Merlin drew closer. He was so keen to learn what had brought Guinevere to the shores of Scotia that his nose was practically inside the sphere of light. The shapes within had taken the form of an old man. Merlin didn't recognise who it was.

The man had a long white beard and misty eyes. He wore a crown, but Merlin had heard that the king of Scotia was in his prime. As he watched the old man talked to someone out of sight, Merlin wondered why Guinevere was interested in this foreign king. Then he saw another man approach the king: this man was younger, tall and thin. He wore a plain brown robe and his deep-set eyes had a wicked glint.

"The first man you saw is Nevan, the king of Eyrieland," Guinevere explained, "I don't know the name of the one who joined him, but he is certainly a sorcerer of considerable power."

Even Happenstance was watching the men closely. The sorcerer bowed and presented something to the king. The old man clapped his hands in excitement. He took in his hands the glowing silver sphere that the sorcerer offered. The shapes dissolved and changed quickly into the castle. Merlin thought that Eyrieland looked even greyer than Scotia.

Soldiers emerged from the castle, dragging out two finely dressed men. They threw both men into the dirt. Giant black birds swooped and dived at the men. Then the castle disappeared, and different scenes came to life in the light, one after another. First of all, Merlin saw a terrific wind tear across a village. Roofs were blown from houses and whole buildings were torn apart. The black birds returned, grown to the size of cattle. They chased children and ruined crops. Strange, shadowy creatures dropped out of the trees. Back in the castle, the king held the sphere tight in his hands, laughing. He looked older than before.

Guinevere dropped her hands and the light disappeared. Happenstance, who had licked his lips hopefully at the sight of the birds, looked disappointed.

"You know where Eyrieland is?" asked Guinevere. Compared to the old king, she looked even taller and more powerful than before.

"Yes, it's the next island to the west. I remember father saying something bad was happening there…"

"He was quite right. A sorcerer presented King Nevan with a gift: a sphere containing some of his own magical power.

But poor King Nevan didn't know, as most people don't, that magic doesn't work that way."

"What do you mean?" Merlin was so absorbed in Guinevere's story that he had forgotten how cold it was.

"Magic has to be earned. If you become my student, I will show you how to earn it. But the sorcerer you saw fooled King Nevan with false promises of power. Magic doesn't take kindly to being cast off and given away. Magic can be vengeful. King Nevan's magic has driven him to madness. He has argued with his sons and sent them into exile. I suspect that the sorcerer is only waiting for him to die before he steps in and takes the throne for himself."

Merlin felt that this was too serious a matter for him to be involved in. "But – how can I help? You should ask the king of Scotia to help King Nevan-"

"I can do more to help than King Stefan. And you will be a great help to me, if you choose to come along."

Happenstance rubbed against Merlin's legs and tried to purr in a soothing way.

"I won't deny that we may see disturbing things in Eyrieland. That sorcerer is aligned with the element of air. You saw for yourself what good that power has brought to the king. His ill-gotten power has called down creatures of shadow from the other world. It has turned ordinary birds into monsters. It has unleashed terrible hurricanes across the island. But poor King Nevan no longer cares about his people. His mind is lost as his greed for power grows. He thinks himself a fearsome sorcerer. Now I hear he uses his power to torment his enemies."

"And what can you do to help?" Merlin was even paler than normal, picturing monsters and hurricanes. "Can you stop the sorcerer taking over Eyrieland?"

"You ask good questions, Merlin." said Guinevere. She smiled across at him. Merlin thought she must be an incredible sorcerer if none of that worried her.

"I plan to take the magic sphere away from the king and destroy it. The magic will be free as soon as the sphere is broken. I can't undo the damage that has already been done, but King Nevan will soon return to normal. He can summon back his sons and guard against the sorcerer."

"Are you sure I'll be able to help?"

"Yes, I'm sure. My attendants here can only follow instructions. I need someone able to think for himself."

Merlin wondered whether he fit that description. Murrow was always saying that he spent too much time in his head. He hoped his father hadn't woken up yet. He wasn't sure what Murrow would make of Guinevere's request that he sail off to Eyrieland. He wasn't sure, either, that he really wanted to meet creatures of shadow from the other world. But how often did sorcerers invite skinny boys like him on adventures? Guinevere smiled as if reading his thoughts.

Chapter Six

Guinevere's Invitation

The sun had already started to rise. Soon there would be no need for Guinevere's magical lights. Guinevere seemed to know, without Merlin saying a word, that he was worried about his father.

"Murrow isn't awake yet," she told him. He didn't ask how she knew his father's name; he felt he'd asked enough questions for one night.

"Now, Merlin, I have a question for you."

Merlin felt Happenstance stand to attention at his side. Even the cat understood that a request from a sorcerer had to be taken seriously.

"I invite you to accompany me to Eyrieland. You know what I plan to do, and what I expect to find there. I won't like and promise you that it will be an easy task, but I believe my powers to be greater than those of the unknown sorcerer."

The first strong beam of sunlight shined down into the valley. Guinevere waved one hand and the lights fell, one by one, into her open palm and burst like bubbles. Merlin watched with an open mouth. He had hardly slept but he was too enlivened by all the night's revelations to long for his bed.

"I won't ask you yet whether you agree to become my student. If you agree to that, you will have to say goodbye to your father and your village for a long time. The journey to obtain magical knowledge will be perilous. I hope you will agree, as I have much to share. But that request will wait for another time. Now, Merlin," she said, her voice growing firm, "I will have you answer my invitation."

Merlin ran a hand through his scraggly blonde hair. He didn't know what to do. He wanted to say yes, but a small part of him still didn't believe he was truly worthy of the invitation. He looked down at Happenstance, who blinked up at him happily.

"Your cat can come, of course," added Guinevere.

Merlin laughed. "Alright, then. Happenstance seems keen on the idea. Yes, I will go with you. I'll try my best to help."

He felt rather embarrassed when she smiled at his answer; he didn't think he'd done much to deserve it yet.

"I am pleased. However, there is one more thing before you can return to your father." Guinevere's eyes flashed in the sunlight. She waved her hand again and drew a small package from her sleeve. The package was tightly wrapped in brown sacking and tied with a cut of rope. Had it not been drawn from the sleeve of a sorcerer it would have looked perfectly ordinary.

"This is not a test of magical skill. All I ask is that you deliver this package to the farmhouse over the next hill. An old friend of mine lives there. You must not get distracted or lose interest in your task. And, most importantly, you must not open the package. Don't stay too long once you've delivered it. My old friend can be quite talkative."

Merlin thought that this task sounded much more significant than Guinevere would have him believe. His hands were shaking slightly as he took the package from the Lady. It felt oddly warm to the touch.

"Where was it you said? A farmhouse?"

"Yes," answered Guinevere, whose face looked much more serious now, "Take the package to the farmhouse over the next hill." She raised a slim hand to point out of the woods. "My old friend will be expecting you."

Happenstance stretched and meowed hungrily.

"You should take Happenstance home for some breakfast. Once you complete your task, come to the harbour. I will be waiting for you. You can tell your father everything I've told you."

Merlin nodded nervously at the lady and bent down to scoop up his cat. He smiled in farewell at Guinevere, his mind swimming with questions. Before he turned away, Guinevere called, "Don't forget my instructions, Merlin. Give my best to Murrow."

The boy smiled in response. He began to climb back up the slope. Happenstance, as usual, was oblivious of his own weight and purred happily in his owner's arms. Merlin turned back for another look at the strange sorcerer but found that she and her attendants had already disappeared.

The walk back to the cottage felt much quicker than the journey into the woods he'd taken the night before. He was almost just as afraid of what awaited him at home – he really hoped his father wasn't already awake. Merlin knew he wasn't always the son Murrow dreamed of, and disappointing his father was always painful.

Happenstance jumped from his arms once they got closer to home and led the way into the cottage. Merlin gave a sigh of relief to find that his father was still fast asleep, snoring loudly. He felt less relieved, however, when he drew out the mysterious package from his sleeve. He set it down on the table, reciting Guinevere's instructions in his head. He hoped he wouldn't forget anything important.

Happenstance felt very pleased with himself for introducing his owner to the Lady Guinevere. He was rewarded with a fish skin for his efforts, and curled up beside the sleeping Murrow. Merlin lit the fire and started to boil water for Murrow's morning tea. They had a great deal to talk about.

Chapter Seven

Merlin's Test Begins

Murrow listened to Merlin's story in disbelief. If what his son said was true, he wasn't certain how much he trusted the Lady. Why should she take such a young boy to battle against a king?

"Are you sure you didn't dream this, Merlin?" he asked, smiling weakly.

"I almost wish I had," answered Merlin, "Things would be much easier then."

"Maybe…but then maybe this is for the best," Murrow started to see Guinevere's request in a new light. He stroked the still-sleeping Happenstance and continued, "You have an opportunity that no-one else in the village has ever been given. I don't know why Guinevere chose you, but she must have seen something in you." He ruffled his son's hair proudly.

Merlin felt much more excited by the prospect of an adventure now that his father approved. He couldn't believe he had considered refusing her request! "So, you think I should go with her?"

"I do, son," smiled Murrow, "Or at least, you should take this test of hers and see what happens. I'll worry about you if you go to Eyrieland, but you'll have a sorcerer on your side."

"But father," Merlin's grin faded, "Won't you be lonely without me?"

"Of course I will. But I have my fishing, and my friends in the village. You'd only be restless if you had to stay here. I can't say it'll be easy, but if Guinevere came all the way to Scotia to find you, then she must know what she's doing."

Merlin hugged his father. He hoped to make him proud. He grabbed the parcel from the table, and called goodbye as he left to make the delivery. He wasn't looking forward to saying a proper goodbye to his father later.

The sky was surprisingly bright that morning. Merlin passed a few villagers as he began his journey. It felt strange to be keeping such a massive secret from the rest of the village. He wondered if they were still discussing Guinevere's arrival in the market yesterday.

The grass tickled his bare feet as he scrambled up the first hill. He held the package tightly in his hand. There was definitely something unusual about its contents: one moment it grew so hot that he struggled to keep a hold of it, then the next it turned as cold as Scotian rain. He wondered how Guinevere came to have an old friend living on the outskirts of the village. He had never even heard of a farmhouse over the hill. When he reached the top of the first hill, he peered into the distance and found what had to be his destination. The farmhouse looked perfectly normal, as far as Merlin could see.

He was half-afraid that some hideous beast would appear and try to steal the package from him. He couldn't understand why just making a delivery counted as a test. Even though Guinevere had said it wasn't a test of magical skill, he was still a bit worried he'd be expected to demonstrate some kind of hidden strength. Merlin glanced around as he started to climb the second hill, but there was no-one nearby.

With a loud *thunk*, the package fell from his hand onto the ground. Merlin was sure he hadn't dropped it. When he bent down to retrieve it, the package began to shake. He thought it must contain a highly powerful magical object to have such a strong will of its own. Merlin remembered, however, his instruction not to be tempted to open it. He grabbed it tightly in his hand again and continued to ascend the hill.

He passed clucking chickens as he drew closer to the farmhouse. It was small and quiet. He wasn't sure if the farmer was at home. Nervously he called out, "Is anyone there? I have a package for you from the Lady Guinevere."

Almost instantly, the farmhouse door creaked open. A small old woman poked out her head. She looked Merlin up and down before shuffling outside. She was even smaller than him. The old woman looked nothing like Merlin had pictured Guinevere's old friend; he had imagined someone much more intimidating. But then, he supposed he didn't look much like a friend of Guinevere's either.

"What does the Lady have for me?" asked the old woman in a croaky voice. She looked greedily at the package Merlin held.

"I don't know what it is," he answered. He was wary of her expression but remembered Guinevere's instructions: he lifted up the package and she grabbed it from him.

"Come in, boy. What do they call you, eh?"

"I'm Merlin," he said.

"Don't just stand there, Merlin. Come in and have a drink. You'll need a rest before you go traipsing back down that hill. It's the least I can do."

She nodded at him encouragingly and waved him inside the farmhouse with a wrinkled hand.

Inside the farmhouse it was almost completely dark. The windows were closed over with shutters and the only light came from a small candle on the table. Guinevere's old friend shuffled towards the table, eagerly unwrapping the package as she moved. Merlin didn't want to spend too much time away from Murrow, but he was curious about the package. He followed the old woman towards the table and asked, "How do you know Guinevere?"

The old woman gave a cackle. "That's too dark a story to share with you, my boy. Come here and have a look at this. I bet you wish you'd had a peek at it on the way here, eh?"

Merlin didn't see what was supposed to be so tempting about the package's contents. A blue orb lay innocently on the wrappings. Merlin then remembered the orb that the sorcerer had presented to King Nevan – this one looked similar. Was Guinevere giving her old friend some of her own magical power?

Chapter Eight

A Vision of Darkness

The old woman cradled the orb in her wizened hands. Merlin couldn't help but ask "What is that?"

"Did Guinevere not tell you anything?"

Merlin shook his head.

"I'll show you what this is." She held it out to him. She looked feeble and not at all threatening but Merlin, thinking of King Nevan, hesitated.

"Can't you just tell me?"

The old woman cackled again. "You're a crafty one, aren't you? I see why Guinevere sent you. Has she told you much about magic, Merlin?"

"No, not much, I suppose…" answered Merlin. He glanced between her face and the blue orb, which had begun to sparkle.

"There are many kinds of magic, Merlin. I specialise in the kind of magic your Guinevere frowns upon. Have you ever lost anyone, eh, anyone close to you?"

"Yes, I suppose…My mother died when I was a baby. But what's that to do with-"

"There's a kind of magic which can help people like you. I can raise the spirits of the dead and reunite boys like you with their loved ones."

She held out the orb again, and this time Merlin accepted it.

"My kind of magic can give you great power. Only the best sorcerers can channel dark magic. Guinevere must have seen something in you, to give you this orb."

"She gave it to you..." corrected Merlin, but he didn't hand it back.

"Have a close look at that orb, Merlin. It'll show you."

Merlin brought it close to his face. The surface changed to show his reflection, before his pale face changed into that of a woman. It had to be his mother: she was pale and blonde like Merlin, just like his father always said. She reached out a hand to him and smiled sadly.

Next, Merlin saw himself. Only this time, he was years older. He was dressed in fine clothes like Guinevere and held a staff like King Nevan. He was leading an army of attendants like Guinevere's, only his were made of fire. They wore no cloaks or hoods, and danced proudly behind

51

their master. Merlin's army of fiery attendants scorched the grass as they marched. When Merlin-in-the-orb gave the command, they sparked and doubled in size, and surged forward to engulf his faceless enemies.

Merlin gasped and dropped the orb. Just before it shattered on the ground, he felt a sharp pain on the back of his hand. As the orb split apart with a loud *crack*, Merlin looked at his hand. A livid red scar had appeared on his skin.

He looked up, but the old woman was no longer in front of him. He heard a sound like a gust of wind, and then the farmhouse was gone, too. He stood alone on top of the hill.

"Well done, Merlin," called a voice behind him.

Merlin jumped. He turned to find Guinevere sweeping towards him, wearing an elusive smile.

"Was that the test?"

Guinevere nodded and lifted his hand to inspect the scar. "Only one strike? You did well to resist the orb's vision."

Merlin felt completely lost. One strike? "Who was that old woman? Was she real or-"

"You ask good questions. But I'm sure you can make sense of it by yourself. I'll be waiting at the harbour for you…and Happenstance, of course."

Guinevere disappeared like the old woman before her. There were no footsteps on the grass where she had stood.

Merlin's hand was still smarting. He took a closer look at the scar he'd earned that morning. He had stayed too long in the farmhouse, listening to false promises of dark magic. He didn't want to end up like the mad king of Eyrieland. He blew onto the scar, hoping his breath would soothe the burning.

"Don't worry. It will fade in time." Guinevere's voice sang in his ear. He whirled around, but he was still alone on the hill.

Chapter Nine

Farewell to Murrow

Murrow helped Merlin wash the scar on his hand while he listened to the tale of the dark orb. Now that his trial was over, Merlin felt invigorated at the prospect of setting sail with Guinevere. He had recovered enough from his broken night of sleep to fully appreciate the wonder of what had happened to him. His father, on the other hand, wasn't sure he liked Guinevere's illusions.

"I hope you don't add any more scars to your collection on your travels," said Murrow.

He was wrapping up a bundle of Merlin's belongings: a pile of clothes, salted fish, and toys he'd carved years ago.

"I won't", answered Merlin, rubbing his hand, "I definitely won't forget any of Guinevere's instructions again."

"I'll be proud of you whatever happens."

Murrow, who was much taller and stronger than Merlin, hugged his son and lifted him off his feet. "The whole village will be whispering about you next."

"So no-one else knows but us?"

"No-one at all. It's weird to have such a big secret, isn't it? Now, where's that cat?"

Reluctant to say goodbye, Merlin and Murrow had shared lunch in the cottage before they started packing. Happenstance, who was dreaming of fat, tasty birds, wasn't pleased with all the activity and had sloped off outside. Thankfully he hadn't wandered too far. Merlin found him snoring in the grass nearby. His jet-black fur didn't make great camouflage.

Murrow caught up with them and clapped his son firmly on the shoulder.

"Here we go, then. I hope I can have a word with the Lady before she whisks you off."

"She might just disappear," said Merlin, lifting up the yawning cat, "She's made it a bit of a habit."

Father and son walked down into the village. As they came closer to the harbour, they were able to see Guinevere's ship. Merlin still couldn't believe he had been invited onto it. He only hoped it was more comfortable than his father's fishing boat.

One of the fishermen, sitting outside his cottage, called to Murrow, "We've not seen a hide of that sorcerer today. I might try to get a closer look at that ship of hers."

"You won't have long to look at it, I'm afraid. Merlin here tells me the Lady is sailing for Eyrieland today."

"Oh really?" The fisherman looked at Merlin with great interest. "How did you hear that?"

Merlin didn't know where to start. He was relieved when Murrow answered for him.

"The Lady summoned him herself. He's been invited to join her." Murrow smiled down at his son.

"Really?" said the fisherman, his eyes wide. He examined Merlin's skinny frame, and said, "Blimey…things just keep getting stranger, don't they?"

He stared at Murrow's face for a moment as if to check he wasn't being tricked, and continued, "Well, best of luck to you, then, Merlin. Make your village proud." He rose to his feet and clasped Merlin's hand.

His neighbours flocked over to see what all the fuss was about. Soon Merlin found himself surrounded by villagers, including the other children who normally overlooked him. Everyone seemed unable to help but scrutinize the pale, thin boy that Guinevere had chosen. Most of the villagers wished him well, and some even presented him with supplies for the journey, but a few looked at him suspiciously. Merlin wondered if they feared he'd returned as a dark enchanter. Everyone wanted to hear that he'd be back as soon as possible so they could hear all about the Lady's errand.

At last, he and Murrow reached the harbour. Out of nowhere, four of Guinevere's blue-faced attendants appeared before them. The crowd behind shrieked to see the old creatures again. The attendants moved aside as Merlin and his father stepped onto the pier, but they slid back into place before anyone else could follow.

Guinevere's tall ship loomed larger than before as they neared it. Before Merlin could get a close look at it, Guinevere stepped down onto the pier and waved in welcome. Happenstance leapt from Merlin's arms to greet her. Murrow approached more cautiously. He wished he could question her about her plans for Merlin, but he didn't expect sorcerers were used to dealing with concerned parents. He didn't want to be cursed for his nosiness.

Another of Guinevere's attendants appeared behind Murrow and, taking the bundle of Merlin's belongings, shuffled onto the ship. Merlin turned and gave his father a final hug.

"Good luck!" said Murrow. He wiped his eyes and looked over to the sorcerer.

Guinevere bowed her head to him and said, "He will be under my protection."

Murrow could only nod in response. Close up, it was difficult not to be awed by the power Guinevere radiated.

Quick as a flash, the attendants shuffled abroad and the ship, its sails fluttering in the wind, left the village harbour. Merlin waved with both hands as his father grew smaller and smaller, and Happenstance meowed in farewell.

Chapter Ten

The Voyage to Eyrieland

Merlin remembered what Guinevere had said about her affinity with water. He was sure that, without the blue attendants, their journey would be much less comfortable. Having spent his entire young life in the village, he wasn't by any means an expert on geography, but he roughly knew that Eyrieland was roughly ten days' journey away. Guinevere's ship, however, flowed smoothly over the waves as if it was part of the ocean itself. The ship was equipped with a steering wheel and a compass, and lots of useful-looking bits of rope, but Merlin had no idea how any of it worked. The attendants stood all around the deck of the ship. No one touched the wheel or peered at the compass. The ship sailed forward without the crew doing anything to help.

"Did you bring food for yourself and Happenstance?" asked Guinevere once the village disappeared from view.

Merlin found it quite frightening not to be able to see land. Guinevere didn't seem to mind at all.

"Yes, Murrow helped me back a few things."

"That's good. I don't think I have enough to fill the stomach of a growing boy. And your cat's stomach looks even bigger."

Happenstance rolled onto his back to show off the belly in question. Merlin was sure cats were supposed to be afraid of water. This reminded him of something he'd meant to ask before.

"How did Happenstance tell you about me?"

"He chose you as his owner. No cat worth his whiskers would choose an owner without some sympathy for the magical arts."

Merlin wasn't sure this answered his question, but Guinevere spoke again.

"I hope the vision I sent you in the orb didn't frighten you too much. I had to be certain you wouldn't be tempted to follow the same path as King Nevan. Otherwise, I would have to steer you away from magic altogether."

The vision of himself as a tyrant had frightened him, but he nodded to show he understood her reasoning. He wondered how many more scars he'd had if he'd opened the package on his way to the farmhouse.

"Oh, I knew you wouldn't be tempted so easily," smiled Guinevere.

Merlin stood silently, piecing the puzzle of the test together.

When he next looked up, Guinevere had gone inside the cabin. Merlin followed, and was faced with a table covered in bundles of flowers and herbs. There were barrels he supposed must contain food, and in the corner hung a small hammock. Underneath the hammock he found his bundle of belongings, and an extra set of blankets. Happenstance pottered in behind him to inspect his new living quarters. There was a door nearby, which he thought must lead to Guinevere's private room. He didn't want to disturb her, just in case she changed her mind about bringing him along. He found a piece of string and began to play with Happenstance, who tried to catch it while moving as little as possible.

Merlin only started to feel sea-sick while he lay in his hammock that night. Happenstance wasn't too happy either and climbed up onto Merlin's chest for comfort. The wind whistled so loudly that they both struggled to fall asleep.

In the morning, he shared a piece of salted fish with the cat. Happenstance was content to take a second nap, but Merlin, worried that the ship was rocking more than the day before, went to look outside.

He gasped – they were already close to land! There was no doubt that Guinevere must be a terrific sorcerer. Eyrieland didn't look threatening yet. All he could see was the rough outline of hills and a rocky shoreline. The sail was shuddering against the torrent of wind.

Guinevere stood beneath the towering sail. She was dressed in a fine white gown and had her head bowed in concentration. Merlin was worried he'd be blown off the ship if the wind kept up.

"You remember what element the sorcerer who fooled King Nevan was aligned with?"

"Oh...it was air! You mean *he's* doing this?" Merlin shivered, wrapping his arms around himself. "He's attacking us?"

He hadn't learned anything about magic yet – he'd have to hide back inside if the sorcerers started to fight.

"He left this part of the world as soon as he left the king, but I have no doubt he's keeping a close eye on things." Guinevere pushed back her long sleeves and waved her hands. "Tie yourself onto the mast with that rope there. Just to be sure," she smiled, when Merlin started.

He quickly did as he was told, too apprehensive to ask any more questions.

The Lady raised her hands high above her head and in front of them a great wave rose in a twisting spiral of water. Faster and faster it spun, and when Guinevere dropped her hands it sprayed in all directions. The wind was taken by surprise by this attack; for a moment it dropped completely. Then the wind returned, stronger and colder than before. Merlin was sure he'd have been lifted off his feet if he wasn't tied to the ship.

Guinevere was not so easily defeated. She raised her hands again and again, until the ship was entirely surrounded by pillars of water. These tall, twisting spirals sheltered them from the wind. The ship continued to race forward smoothly across the waves, and the defeated wind could only whine in the distance.

Chapter Eleven

Merlin and Guinevere Go Ashore

Happenstance poked his furry face round the cabin door. He didn't look too happy about the waves that surrounded them. Merlin was glad the journey had turned out to be a short one. Although he knew what awaited them in Eyrieland, he was still looking forward to walking on solid ground again. He beamed up at Guinevere, in awe of her magic. She swept across to undo the rope.

"We'll reach land soon. I'm aiming for a little beach out of the way. I hope we can learn more about the situation before anyone becomes suspicious."

As the ship sailed on, Merlin could see a sheltered, pebbled beach ahead. He was surprised at how similar Eyrieland looked to his home country. He had expected a foreign land to look a bit more *foreign*. He wished he'd asked before whether any dangerous animals lived there, but then he remembered the giant birds and shadowy creatures, and decided that they already had enough to worry about.

As the ship started to slow down, Happenstance came out to join them. He looked gloomily up at the gathering rainclouds. Merlin was caught by surprise when Guinevere's attendants began to leap from the ship into the water, each one landing with a soft splash. He gave her a questioning look. She pointed ahead to the shore. The attendants appeared rose, one by one, out of the tide and took on their solid shapes again. Merlin hoped she wasn't expecting him and Happenstance to swim to shore.

He knew enough about sailing to know that ships as large as Guinevere's couldn't go in too close to the shore in case they hit against rocks. Guinevere's ship, however, kept going until it slowed to a halt on the beach.

"We can leave our belongings here," said Guinevere, "My attendants will guard the ship."

As she spoke, the blue creatures gathered around the ship until they circled it completely. Guinevere turned and walked off the ship – Merlin was convinced she'd jumped and ran behind to see. Instead he found a neat set of steps he was sure hadn't been there before.

With a loud meow, Happenstance leapt up onto his shoulder. Merlin hoped the cat knew what he was getting himself in for. He clambered down the steps after Guinevere.

Together Merlin and Guinevere walked across the beach, the pebbles crunching beneath their feet. Merlin followed her up a narrow path and they wound across the grassy dunes. Rain began to fall, lightly at first, but soon the storm grew stronger. The sky was shrouded by clouds. Happenstance burrowed in close to Merlin. Apart from the splashing rain drops, there was not a sound to be heard.

As they passed by a withered tree, Merlin heard a loud squawking from above. He looked up and saw an evil-looking bird glaring down from the topmost branch. He wished that Guinevere had told him exactly what she expected him to do.

He felt younger than eleven when they reached the first village. It frightened him to see how similar the village was to the one he had left behind – expect this one was dreadfully changed.

"Was this the village you showed me in the woods?"

"The wind has definitely struck this place."

Guinevere stopped to take a look around them. She was already soaked. Merlin thought he must look like a drowned rat. Guinevere's fine dress didn't seem to absorb the water like his clothes did.

The remains of a row of cottages stood nearby. The roofs were missing from them all, and the walls had started to collapse.

"Does anyone still live here?" asked Merlin nervously.

"Yes, the villagers are still here," answered Guinevere, as she began to walk ahead again. Merlin wondered how she knew, as he couldn't see or hear anyone nearby.

They passed a heap of rubble and broken barrels of good. There were more abandoned cottages. As they walked, birds began to caw loudly above them. Thankfully, none were as large as the birds he'd seen in the woods that night (which already felt like a lifetime ago).

Guinevere quickly turned between two cottages. She waved for Merlin and Happenstance to follow. Merlin stepped carefully over the broken stones as she led him towards a small paddock.

When Merlin caught up with her he couldn't quite believe his eyes. A group of some fifty people were huddled together in the centre of the field. Small children cried, while the adults either sat or stood with their heads in their hands. Merlin couldn't figure out what they were doing there; no-one was forcing them to stay there, yet they were acting like prisoners. He tried to take a step towards them, but Guinevere stopped him.

"You should stand back, Merlin." There was no trace of fear in Guinevere's voice.

Merlin stepped back and gave Happenstance a reassuring pat.

Guinevere unlatched the gate and strode across the field. The villagers called out to her: some begged for help, while others looked terrified and warned her to turn back. Merlin couldn't see her face but imagined that she was smiling mysteriously at the villagers.

As Guinevere continued to stride across the field, a flash of lightning broke across the sky. Merlin whispered soothingly to the cat perched on his shoulder as the rain splashed down around them.

Chapter Twelve

Creatures of Shadow

Guinevere was only a few feet away from the huddling villagers when something started to happen. The villagers began to cry and shout in warning. At first Merlin couldn't see what was going on. Soon, though, it became horribly clear. Dark shadows grew out of the ground. They stretched up until they were even taller than Guinevere. Merlin thought they looked more terrifying than the flame creatures he had seen in the orb. They had no eyes, but Merlin could tell that their attention was focused on Guinevere. The shadow creatures advanced towards the sorcerer until she was surrounded. Some of the villagers looked away, too afraid to watch.

The thunder rumbled around them. One of the shadow creatures lifted an arm to try and grab Guinevere. She leapt back just in time and its grip closed around thin air. It reached forward again but this time Guinevere stopped it with her own hand. The creature flinched back, but another managed to grab her. It lifted her into the air and quickly threw her aside. Merlin gasped, afraid that she was injured, but Guinevere landed softly on her feet. The villagers began to call out to her again. Merlin guessed that they had now realised she was no ordinary woman.

Guinevere called, "Return to the shadow realm. My power is greater than that which set you loose in these lands. Begone, or I will banish you!"

The shadow creatures didn't flinch. The ground beneath them began to turn black as if the shadows were spreading. Guinevere took a few steps back.

"I'm afraid you won't be able to drag me into your realm. Go back to sleeping beneath the earth, where you belong!"

Guinevere's command rang out strongly. Merlin was completely spellbound by the power she exuded.

The shadow creatures doubled in size as lightning flashed behind them. Their hands snatched at Guinevere like claws but she stood her ground. The sorcerer raised her hands up to the sky.

Merlin stroked a sodden Happenstance as he saw the true depth of Guinevere's powers. She looked taller as she began to chant in a strange language. Her white dress seemed to glow. The clouds began to move across the sky until most of the rain poured directly onto the shadow creatures. They started to shrink back towards the ground.

When one reached towards Guinevere, a glowing blue sword appeared in her hand. She slashed out at the shadow until it sank back into the ground. Guinevere then struck out at the other shadows. She was careful not to step onto the black patch on the ground. When only one shadow remained, Guinevere called, "I banish you and your kind from walking this land!"

The last creature disappeared into the ground. Guinevere commanded the clouds to move back as the sword vanished from her hand. She turned to wave at Merlin, who raced towards her.

The villagers were firing questions at Guinevere when he arrived. A group of children grinned up at Happenstance. The cat licked his paw proudly.

"Thank you for rescuing us! Those demons stole all our possessions and kept us here!" sobbed one villager, while another asked, "Are you a sorcerer? Where did you come from?" Guinevere said that she hoped to find the cause of the country's misery. She waved away the rest of their questions and told them to find shelter from the rain.

"I'll send my attendants along tonight to help repair the damage to the village. It's better not to scare them with too much magic in one day," she told Merlin. "Did you know that people here spoke a different language to you?"

Merlin blinked in surprise. "Oh – but – I could understand them!"

"Yes, indeed," laughed Guinevere. "I enchanted you so that you could understand the people here. We are speaking in Eyrieish right now."

"No, we can't be!" said Merlin, his eyes wide in disbelief.

Guinevere laughed at his expression. She led him back to walk through the rest of the village. The villagers they passed waved over at them and called out words of thanks to the sorcerer.

Chapter Thirteen

Chaos in Castletown

The wind roared around Guinevere and Merlin as they followed a winding road to the next town. Merlin was cradling Happenstance in his arms to stop him being blown away by the wind. At least it wasn't raining anymore, he thought to himself. Guinevere had used her magic to dry his clothes, but he couldn't help but feel the cold.

"We're getting closer to the king," she called over the whistling wind, "But we'll find out what havoc his magic has wreaked in Castletown before we pay him a visit."

Merlin nodded. He hoped he could prove himself useful soon, as he currently felt like he was more useful to Happenstance than to Guinevere.

The sound of raised voices reached them as they entered the town. Every person they could see was embroiled in an argument, shouting, screaming or stomping their feet in rage at their neighbours. Every face wore a scowl. One man caught Merlin looking at him and screeched, "What do you think you're looking at?!!" Another shouted at Guinevere "Who do you think you are to dress so proudly?"

In the marketplace, the townsfolk browsing at the stalls squabbled over the goods on sale. No-one was immune to the dark mood in the town.

Guinevere led Merlin out of sight and said, "I suspect the townsfolk here have been infected by the king's magic. They live too close to the castle to be spared from his curse. Can you do something for me, Merlin?"

"Yes," said Merlin, standing to attention. He was eager to prove himself – and relieved that his task was unlikely to involve battling the shadow creatures.

"I want you to talk to the townsfolk here, one at a time. See if you can figure out what's causing them all to be so angry with one another."

Merlin was surprised that she asked him to do this, as he was sure she'd be able to solve the townsfolk's problems with just a wave of her hand. He kept this thought to himself, however, and promised to try his best. Guinevere lifted Happenstance from his arms and told him she'd be watching.

He talked to a merchant first. The merchant was selling hand-carved toys, which reminded Merlin of home. He asked why the merchant scowled at everyone who passed, and the man replied, rolling his eyes, "Because every customer is a thief, of course!"

Merlin blinked, then asked when something had last been stolen from him. The merchant had to think about this for a good long while. Eventually he met Merlin's eyes and said that he couldn't remember. In fact, he wasn't sure he'd ever been stolen from at all. Suddenly, he looked much happier. He began to call out to the crowd to advertise his goods.

Merlin bumped into a woman as he turned away. She looked down her rather beaky nose at the small boy and roared "Can't you look where you're going?!"

Merlin offered a meek apology, but she had already started to move on. He called over to her, asking if she was alright. She turned back and he flinched, expecting to be yelled at again, but instead she said quietly "I can't remember the last time someone asked me that."

"You should ask the next person who frowns at you," suggested Merlin, which made her laugh.

He spent the rest of the drizzly afternoon in the marketplace. He convinced feuding families to talk to each other, and they discovered that it had been a misunderstanding all along. He helped repair a stall that had been destroyed by the wind and talked others into lending a hand. The stall owner was so pleased by their generosity that he shook hands with every one of them. Just being smiled at was enough to snap most of the townsfolk out of their foul moods.

It wasn't long before the atmosphere in the marketplace was completely transformed. Merlin hoped this new mood would spread throughout the town. Guinevere swept out of nowhere beside him. Smiling, she offered him a chunk of bread. The cat on her shoulder looked pleased with himself, which could only mean that he'd been fed too.

"How did I do?" asked Merlin nervously. He hoped he wasn't supposed to have tried something magical.

"You were brilliant, Merlin. I was right to bring you here," said Guinevere, with a smile that lit up her eyes. "Now, are you ready to meet the king?"

Chapter Fourteen

An Audience with the King

Merlin had never seen a castle before, but he expected that most castles were more heavily guarded than King Nevan's. The castle itself was quite squat and grey. Soldiers with swords in their belts were patrolling around the entrance. Merlin felt sure he'd be arrested as a foreign spy. Guinevere had asked that he go alone, ahead of her, to request an audience with the king. She believed that the sorcerer who'd tricked King Nevan might have warned the king about her. Merlin thought she was right about that, but wished she'd said more about how he was supposed to act with the king. Was he supposed to bow? What happened if King Nevan tried to curse him?

He approached the castle gate. None of the soldiers seemed very interested in him. One tall soldier was lounging beside the gate and looked up as Merlin drew close. He didn't say anything but Merlin had to make sure he was allowed to pass.

"I've come to see- " he started to tell the soldier, but the man cut him off mid-sentence.

"Do what you like. That mad old fool won't listen to you anyway. He's dismissed half of his advisors and exiled the princes. There's no hope for any of us now."

Merlin was taken aback by the soldier's bitter tone and couldn't quite believe that he'd called his king a 'mad old fool'. At least Merlin wasn't the only one who had no idea how to address the king.

He hurried through the gate and into the castle, glad to escape the rain. The castle was just as grey and gloomy on the inside. He had expected to be met by servants or soldiers, but instead he had to find his own way to the king. He knew he was in the right place when he heard a wavering voice shout, "I knew you were plotting against me from the start! Get out of my castle! Go! Go!"

Merlin had to jump aside as a finely robed man stormed past, cursing the king under his breath. Merlin hadn't been expecting his meeting with the king to go well, but now he was sure Guinevere would have to take the orb by force.

He walked slowly into the throne room. King Nevan sat on his throne, exactly as he had looked in the orb. His misty eyes found Merlin and he called, "What brings you before your king? Have you come to beg from me?"

They were alone in the room. It looked as if all of the king's protectors had deserted him.

"I just came to ask about the wind and the giant birds that have been attacking people. I was wondering whether-"

He was interrupted by the king's hacking cough. "Are you trying to blame your king for the misfortunes of your family? Some might consider that treason."

Merlin spotted the staff, its orb glowing inside, leaning against the throne. He wondered if the king could move fast enough to stop him if he tried to take it. "I just wondered if the orb you have might be causing-"

"Oh, so you've heard of my magical power? And here I thought you were just some peasant boy. You make an excellent spy. Who put you up to this? Who wants to take my power from me?"

In his rage, the king staggered to his feet. Merlin didn't know what to say. It was true that he wanted to take the king's power from him, and technically he was spying for Guinevere…

"Answer me! Don't ignore your king!"

Happenstance meowed in greeting to Merlin, who started. He turned to find Guinevere stroll into the throne room, the cat perched up on her shoulder. Happenstance jumped to the ground, which impressed Merlin, as it was quite a distance from Guinevere's shoulder to the floor, and scampered over to Merlin. Standing tall and proud, Guinevere made a striking contrast with the king.

"Who are you?" shouted the king. He looked so frail that Merlin couldn't help but feel sorry for him. King Nevan grabbed the staff and glared at Guinevere.

Chapter Fifteen

A Flood of Magic

Guinevere bowed her head to the king. "I came here as a friend," she told him, "My name is Guinevere. You may have already been told about me-"

"You're a sorcerer!" interrupted King Nevan. "I have been warned about you! The sorcerer who showed me how to obtain my own power warned me that other, more selfish sorcerers might try to take my powers from me. Yes, I remember your name, *Guinevere*!" He spat out her name like it was poison.

"Who was the sorcerer that gave you your power?" asked Guinevere. She didn't look at all fazed by the king's outburst.

"He told me you might ask!" said the king triumphantly, rocking on his feet. "But I will tell you nothing, false sorcerer. I order you to leave my domain, at once!"

"I'm afraid I cannot leave, your majesty. I am not a threat to your power. I am not nearly as dangerous as the sorcerer who gave you that orb."

She lifted her hand to point to the staff. King Nevan drew it closer to protect it and scowled. Merlin knelt beside Happenstance, prepared to shield the cat if King Nevan started sending his shadow minions or monstrous birds to attack them. Fortunately, it seemed King Nevan had entirely forgotten about him; he had eyes only for Guinevere.

The red-haired sorcerer continued, "Magic cannot simply be given away. Forgive me for saying so, but you have not passed the tests required to prove yourself worthy of magic. As a result, your magic has run rampant and infected your kingdom-"

"Enough!" bellowed the king. "Silence, foul witch! These are lies! How dare you call me, the king of Eyrieland, unworthy! I am a great leader and a powerful sorcerer. I have banished my own sons for speaking ill of my power; do you think I'll hesitate to punish you?"

"Has your magic helped your kingdom? Has it made your life better than it was before?"

"Enough!" cried the king. "I'll show you what I do to those who defy my orders!" He slammed the end of the staff down on the stone floor. As it clunked, silver sparks shot out of the orb.

Merlin smiled in relief, thinking that the king's magic had failed him, but then he saw Guinevere surrounded by shadowy claws, which had slithered up from the ground.

94

They grabbed at her arms and legs and tried to drag her out of the king's presence. She continued to look calmly at the king as they pulled her back.

"You know that I'm telling you the truth: your magic has only caused you grave harm. That sorcerer didn't give you a gift; he gave you a curse!" She raised her hands sharply out of the shadows' reach and summoned the shining blue sword she'd used before. The shadows retreated in fear of it, before she had even struck them.

"You're a lying witch!" sobbed the king.

Merlin could almost feel his desperation. He scooped up Happenstance and took a few steps back, wanting to stay out of the king's line of vision. He moved just in time, as the king pointed his staff at Guinevere and fired a blast of cold air at her. The strength of the current was powerful enough to split open the stone floor. Guinevere jumped aside. For the first time, Merlin thought she looked worried.

"Your magic is powerful, but you are not in control of it. You are a danger to your own kingdom. I cannot allow you to fool yourself any longer!"

Resolved, she threw the blue sword towards the king. Merlin flinched – was she really going to attack him?

In mid-air the sword split apart and its shards turned to water; these drops grew and spread into a terrific wave. The wave expanded further as it rose high in the air, and with an echoing roar it fell upon the king. After a moment, the wave sank into the floor and vanished, exposing a sodden king. Nevan had been knocked to his knees by the force of the water.

Merlin hoped Guinevere's magic had swept away King Nevan's delusion, but he was soon proved wrong. The king snarled at the offending sorcerer and shouted "I am in control of my magic! And I am in control of you!"

Chapter Sixteen

Happenstance Joins the Fray

Guinevere held King Nevan's furious gaze but her pale face was impossible to read. After a moment, she sighed, contemplating the sodden king.

"I assure you that you're not in control of anyone. And you are certainly not in control of yourself. Please, give that staff to me. That sorcerer has poisoned your mind. Haven't you noticed that everything around you has taken a turn for the worse since you were given that orb?"

The king spluttered. "My sons were jealous of my power! They sought to take it from me and claim the throne. My advisors have revealed themselves to be a bunch of fools, plotting against me, and spreading lies about my kingdom!"

He looked utterly mad as he ranted. Merlin wished he was as easy to talk sense into as the townsfolk in the marketplace.

Guinevere said coolly, "Do you think that you have great magical power?"

"Yes!" shouted the king, "I have tremendous-"

"Did your friend the sorcerer," she cut across him, "explain what true magic is capable of?"

"Yes, he did! And I have seen for myself what my magic can do!" The king smirked at Guinevere smugly.

"Magic is capable of great things in the hands of a real sorcerer. If you haven't earned your magic, it will take over. Watch carefully. I will show you what true magic can do."

She whistled. Happenstance meowed and took a few plodding steps towards her. Without moving a muscle, Guinevere cast her magic over the cat. Merlin watched, aghast, as his beloved pet grew in all directions: his paws grew to the size of small dogs, his claws became monstrously sharp, and his body stretched until he was the height of Guinevere, and much wider, and his furry face became fearsome when his massive mouth opened, revealing pointed fangs.

The gigantic Happenstance turned to Merlin. He meowed proudly before hissing at the king. Merlin thought that Guinevere must have somehow explained her ploy to Happenstance, because he was doing an excellent job at showing off her magical skill. The monstrous Happenstance took a step towards the king. Nevan looked horrified. Merlin couldn't help but feel a wave of sympathy for him. He looked far too old and frail to be battling against Guinevere's magic.

"You are a demon!" he shouted. "Your magic must be evil to have created this beast!"

"My magic is powerful. It is neither good nor evil. But I do have a conscience, unlike magic. Please, your highness, you have placed your trust in the wrong person. That orb has caused you nothing but harm."

But the king merely shook his head. He was shaking as he stared at Happenstance. Merlin couldn't blame him; he would be quivering himself if Happenstance had been facing him. While Happenstance lifted one massive paw to clean between his claws, the king lifted up his staff.

"I have dark creatures of my own! No one has greater magic than mine!" He waved the staff in the air, and Merlin heard what sounded like a flurry of wings nearby.

Cawing and shrieking, a flock of those oversized black birds fluttered into the room. They were much bigger than Merlin. As one bounded towards him, he backed away quickly. Its beak looked as sharp as a scythe. Another bird was circling Guinevere, flapping its wings and cawing at her menacingly. The third bird, the largest of them all, swept down at Happenstance to nip his shoulder with its clawed feet. Happenstance let out a shriek. King Nevan laughed, but stopped smirking once Happenstance rose up on his back paws and batted the bird away.

The bird nearest Merlin continued to hop towards him. Its head was tilted to one side. Merlin didn't fancy being nipped by that beak. He met the bird's glinting eyes and wished that he had magic, too. He felt very aware of how small and skinny and young he was. Suddenly, he felt a burning strength inside him, red hot in his chest: '*I have been useful to Guinevere. She wouldn't waste her time on me if I was really useless to her…* ' He took a step forward towards the bird. It cawed again, in a questioning sort of way, before flying over towards Happenstance.

Like its brother, the bird dove down at the gigantic cat and tried to nip with his beak. Happenstance was prepared this time. He had the same transfixed look on his face as when Merlin teased him with bits of string. The giant cat swatted away the pestering birds.

Guinevere lifted up her hand so that the palm faced towards the bird flapping around her. A jet of water shot out from her hand, soaking the creature. It turned away, and landed with its fellows beside the king. They began to peck at his robes in a menacing way.

"Send them away," called Guinevere, "And I will return the cat to his usual size."

"Alright," croaked the king. He was exhausted. He couldn't believe that his magic had failed him. With sagging shoulders, he shooed away the birds. They were reluctant to leave, but eventually they took flight and swept out of the room.

"My apologies, Merlin," said Guinevere, smiling at him, "I hope you don't mind me borrowing your cat."

Happenstance had already started to shrink. In a few blinks of an eye, he had returned to the small, furry, round form that Merlin knew and loved.

"Not at all," he grinned, hurrying across to pet Happenstance.

Chapter Seventeen

The Sorcerer Speaks

The king sank down onto his throne. His hands shook as he examined the staff. Guinevere began to walk towards him.

"I don't know who that sorcerer was, but he is a dangerous man. Don't blame yourself too harshly for this, your majesty. Magic can corrupt the best of us."

"But I had such power!" croaked the king. "Why should I trust you? Everyone wants to take my power away!" He began to sob. Merlin felt this difficult to watch. Steeling himself, he lifted up Happenstance and went to stand beside Guinevere.

"You were a great king until you were offered that orb. The promise of magic made you greedy, and in your greed you were blinded to the darkness which swept across your kingdom," Guinevere spoke calmly, "But you can become a great king again. Please, give up your dream of magic. Give that orb to me so that I can destroy it. Bring your sons home."

King Nevan continued to cry. After a moment, he wiped his eyes and nodded. "Alright. I give in. I'll give up my orb. Here, take it."

He held out the staff. Guinevere approached the throne. When she was only a step away, her hand outstretched, smoke began to pour out from the orb. The king started and dropped the staff. Guinevere said, "It seems your sorcerer has been keeping an eye on things."

"What is it doing?" asked the king, as the orb began to glow. Merlin suspected that even Guinevere wasn't sure what was going to happen.

The smoke billowed away. Then a voice began to speak to them from the orb. Its accent was strange to Merlin's ears (he still had a hard time accepting that he was speaking in Eyrieish) but different to Guinevere's accent. Merlin imagined a voice like that belonging to someone old, tall and bearded, and powerful like Guinevere.

"So you came, Guinevere. I warned you, King Nevan, that other sorcerers might be drawn to your power…"

"A desperate attempt to trick the king. You have already lost," answered Guinevere, frowning at the orb.

Ignoring her, the voice continued. "Who is the boy you've brought along? He's too young to be joining you on your…*adventures*. Do you plan to teach him about magic? What a waste of time."

Merlin felt like stamping on the orb. He burst out, "Who are you?"

The strange sorcerer laughed. "So there's fire in you, after all. I am a sorcerer. But you have no need to know about me. I have no interest in Guinevere's playthings."

"You have no business with him," said Guinevere sharply. She placed a hand on Merlin's shoulder to comfort him. "You've been exposed as a trickster. The king will no longer be under the influence of your foul magic."

She took a step forward. The orb hissed, and the voice laughed again. "You had better stop interfering in my business, my Lady, or one day soon we'll meet in person."

Guinevere didn't bother to respond. She stamped firmly down on the orb. With a final burst of smoke, the orb cracked. King Nevan cried out as the magic left him. Then, he slumped back on his throne, a tired old man. When he looked up, his eyes were less misty than before. Guinevere lifted up the staff to remove the broken orb. It turned to dust in her hand. The king watched her nervously, as if afraid she was going to shout at him.

"How do you feel, your highness?" asked Merlin.

King Nevan looked up at the pale boy. "I feel very tired. Would you send a message for me, Lady Guinevere? I think it's high time I brought my sons home."

Chapter Eighteen

Revival

The deserted castle quickly sprang to life again. Disgruntled soldiers returned to welcome back their king. Advisors and officials wept with joy to have their noble leader returned to them. Merlin, Guinevere and Happenstance kept the king company throughout all the activity. Merlin was still slightly wary of the king, but Nevan was trying hard to make amends. He had succeeded in befriending Happenstance, who purred proudly on the king's lap.

Guinevere asked the king to make a promise: "If you ever hear about that sorcerer again, will you tell me?"

"Yes, my Lady," he said, "But where will I find you?"

"It's enough that you've promised. Trust me, I'll know."

They shook hands. King Nevan still looked a bit afraid of Guinevere. Merlin couldn't really blame him. Guinevere had definitely proved how powerful her magic was. He thought it strange that Guinevere was so mysterious, even when speaking to a king – she told King Nevan nothing about herself. It was as though she feared no-one. Merlin rather liked that about her.

They heard all about King Nevan's plans to repair his kingdom. He ordered messengers to be sent to every village in the kingdom to share the good news. He was inspired by the story of how Merlin had overpowered the dark mood in Castletown and instructed his soldiers to settle every argument they overheard. Already Eyrieland felt like a completely new place.

After a long while, Guinevere turned to Merlin and smiled. "Would you like to go home soon, Merlin?"

"Yes, if that's okay," he said, feeling slightly embarrassed. He didn't want her to think he was homesick already.

"We've done all we can to help here," she answered.

King Nevan showered them with his gratitude. They were offered warm clothes and food for their journey back to Scotia but Guinevere said they had everything they would need. King Nevan then said, "I would like to name both of you as Protectors of the Realm."

The crowd that had gathered in the throne room burst into applause. Merlin felt his face burn with pride. He didn't understand what that meant but knew he had been awarded a great honour.

Guinevere placed a hand on his shoulder. "So young, and you've already earned a title. Your father will be proud."

Merlin's cheeks soon hurt from grinning so widely.

Surrounded by admirers, Guinevere and Merlin departed from the castle. Happenstance perched on Merlin's shoulder, lapping up all the attention. He didn't seem to mind missing out on his usual day-long nap. The marketplace, when they reached it, was much busier than before. Merlin had gifts of food and sweets pressed into his hands.

At the outskirts of Castletown they waved goodbye to their followers. They fell silent as they began to walk back to the ship. After a pause, Guinevere said, "I won't ask you yet whether you'd like to learn more about magic. But I hope you understand that magic isn't anything to be afraid of. Like any kind of power, it can be good or evil depending on who wields it."

"I think I understand," he said, then continued, feeling brave, "Your magic is incredible. Can you show me more?"

Guinevere laughed softly. Happenstance toyed with a strand of Merlin's straw-coloured hair before settling down to sleep.

When they passed through the village, Merlin was pleased to see that the villagers had already started to rebuild their homes. The villagers called out and waved to the tall woman and the small boy as they passed.

On the pebbly beach, Guinevere's servants stood waiting. They hadn't moved an inch all day. The sky was growing dark but with a wave of her hand a lantern appeared in Guinevere's grasp. She helped Merlin to climb up the steps to the ship.

"Will the sorcerer attack you with the wind again?" he asked.

"I don't think so. He's probably busy somewhere else by now."

"How many sorcerers are there in the world?" asked Merlin. He was alive with excitement. He was going home to tell Murrow all about his adventures!

Guinevere whispered under her breath. In answer to her command, the ship lunged forward and began to glide across the turbulent sea.

"There are others," she said vaguely, turning back to face him. "But I have a question for you: would you mind meeting another king?"

This question caught Merlin completely by surprise. He started, causing Happenstance to meow huffily on his shoulder.

"An-another king?" he stammered.

"Yes," smiled Guinevere, "*Your* king, in fact. I promised King Stefan of Scotia that I'd visit him again one day."

"Wow…." replied Merlin. He wondered if every sorcerer held as many secrets as Guinevere.

Chapter Nineteen

A Royal Welcome

Merlin stayed awake all night. Happenstance lay stretched out at his feet, snoring happily, but Merlin sat up looking at the twinkling sky above. A cool breeze swept around him but Guinevere had been right about the defeated sorcerer: there was no magical battle of wits that night. Guinevere whiled away the hours inside the cabin, while her servants kept watch over Merlin outside.

At long last he saw his homeland in the distance. As the veil of darkness lifted, revealing a sky streaked with pale pink and blue, Merlin stood up to peer across the waves to Scotia. While he knew it was just an island, and while he knew it looked almost exactly the same as Eyrieland, to Merlin it was *home*. His heart swelled with joy to see it again.

The sun had fully risen by the time they reached the rocky shore. Guinevere called good morning as she joined him on deck. Her robe was now sapphire blue. Merlin hoped King Stefan wouldn't mind how plain he looked. While he was excited to meet the king, he was also worried about offending him, and most of all, he wanted to share the details of his eventful day in Eyrieland before he began to forget them.

Guinevere led him down onto the beach. He had to carry Happenstance, who was determined to make up for the sleep he'd missed.

"You should have slept, Merlin," she told him, but she didn't seem angry. "I hope you're awake enough to enjoy this. You said you'd like to see more magic?"

She raised her hands and Merlin gasped to see the strength of her skill. The beautiful ship they had travelled in began to fold in upon itself, its sail collapsing into the deck, and with a thud, a crash, and a wallop, it had sorted itself out into the shape of a carriage. It looked fit for royalty.

Merlin grinned, "That was brilliant!"

Guinevere laughed. Around them half of the blue-faced servants began to change, too. Unlike the ship, they sprouted rather than shrank. They grew into the shape of six massive blue horses. Their capes then grew, too, to cover most of the strangeness of their appearance.

"They will take us quickly to the castle," explained Guinevere. "And the rest can keep us company inside."

She led Merlin to the carriage door. He climbed inside to find two comfy rows of cushioned seats. Guinevere sat across from him and Happenstance by the window, and the servants followed suit. Quick as a flash, the makeshift horses began to pull the carriage across the beach. Merlin found the bumpiness of the carriage quite soothing. Before he could stop himself, he had fallen fast asleep.

The carriage bustled along the winding roads. The skies were grey and heavy with rain. Neither the pattering of the rain or the trundling of the carriage was enough to wake Merlin up. Guinevere had to give him a shake before he opened his eyes. She told him to look out the window. When he looked he couldn't quite believe his eyes. A grand castle waited for them ahead. The red and blue flag of Scotia waved proudly all around the road. Merlin's heart seemed to be trying to leap out of his chest. Somehow the prospect of meeting his king was more frightening than facing dark magic.

"King Stefan will be glad to meet you," said Guinevere. "And Happenstance, too, of course," as the cat bristled.

Their carriage was greeted at the castle gates with trumpets. They left behind the servants and followed a servant inside. Happenstance walked in front of Merlin, holding up his tail proudly. Merlin fidgeted, caught between shyness and curiosity. The scene inside the castle could not have been more different to King Nevan's court. King Stefan's castle was crowded with lively, smiling men and women. Guinevere and Merlin were surrounded by a sea of chattering voices.

Once people started to notice the tall figure of Guinevere, the voices turned to whispers instead. The crowd parted to let them through. Merlin soon found himself looking up at the king.

Stefan had long, curly yellow hair, longer even than Guinevere's, with a beard to match. He was tall and looked far healthier than King Nevan. He stood and smiled as they walked towards him. His wife sat on a throne to his left; Merlin had been told that the Queen had jet-black hair. The two royal princesses sat on the Queen's other side, but they were too busy talking happily to each other to notice Guinevere.

Guinevere kneeled down and bowed her head. Merlin quickly copied her – and even Happenstance was polite enough to sit down. He heard a booming laugh and then the king said, "My fair Lady, I hadn't expected you to visit so soon! Rise, rise! And you, too, young sir!"

Chapter Twenty

The King of Scotia

Merlin rose back up on his feet. Nervous as he was, it was impossible not to return King Nevan's smile. It was easy to see why he was such a popular king. Stefan leaned forward, hands on his knees, to take a good look at Merlin. "And what can I call you? Are you a Scotian lad?"

"I am, your highness," said Merlin, in a quiet voice. He wondered if anyone in the village would believe his report of meeting the famous king! "My name is Merlin. I come from a fishing village."

"Merlin it is. And Guinevere! You haven't aged a day since I last saw you. People might think you're a sorcerer if you're not careful!" His laugh echoed across the room. Merlin spotted the Queen rolling her eyes in an affectionate sort of way behind him. "And you've brought a cat along. Or is this how you punish your enemies?" joked the king as he stroked Happenstance.

"I'm glad to see you in good humour, your majesty. I'm starting to wish I had come to visit sooner," smiled Guinevere.

"What brings you here today, my Lady?" asked the king. Even though the room was still busy with noise, Merlin was certain that almost everyone was straining to hear their conversation.

"I paid a visit to King Nevan of Eyrieland. You must have heard the rumours…"

"Ah yes! In fact, I thought about you as soon as I heard – I'm grateful that the message reached you so quickly."

Merlin thought that King Stefan must be used to Guinevere's way of knowing absolutely everything; either that or he was good at hiding his surprise.

"Yes," smiled Guinevere, "And every rumour was true. Another sorcerer tricked King Nevan with false promises of magic. I believe he meant to have King Nevan drag the whole kingdom into ruin before stepping in to save the day and claim the throne for himself."

"So we were dangerously close to having a dark sorcerer for our neighbour. You managed to save not one but two kingdoms, my Lady."

"You are very kind," replied Guinevere. (Merlin was starting to understand that even sorcerers without king still had to be polite to other people's).

"And is Nevan quite recovered?"

"He will make a full recovery. The princes have been invited back to the castle, and the people are starting to rebuild. I don't know who the sorcerer responsible is, but I think it'll be some time before we hear of him again in this part of the world."

"Marvellous news! You have the gratitude of the Scotian people, my Lady."

The milling crowd burst into applause. Apparently they had given up on pretending not to eavesdrop.

"And how did this young lad come to join you?" asked Stefan. He didn't look too shocked to see that Guinevere had chosen a stringy boy of eleven for her companion, and for that Merlin was grateful.

"I've been looking for a student for some time. I have too much magical knowledge not to share some. Otherwise it might start to leak," she smiled, "Merlin here agreed to come to Eyrieland and see what he thought of magic."

Merlin felt both proud and embarrassed by Guinevere's description. He was aware that almost every eye in the room was focused on him. Even the princesses were staring. He knew he looked nothing like a sorcerer. Aware that King Stefan was looking at him, Merlin raised his head and gave a sheepish smile. King Stefan took one of Merlin's thin hands in his own and shook it.

"You will make your village very proud, young master Merlin."

Again the room burst with applause. King Stefan laughed to find all of his subjects staring so intently at his guests.

"Don't worry, you'll have plenty of time to stare. I insist that Lady Guinevere, Master Merlin, and their handsome cat, all join us to dine this evening."

Chapter Twenty-One

Knights and Medals

The banquet hall was bigger than any place Merlin had ever seen before. He felt smaller and more invisible than usual. At the same time, however, he somehow also felt more comfortable in his own skin than ever before: he knew how amazingly lucky he was to be invited to dine with the king.

The rain lashed down outside but not loudly enough to interrupt the festivities. The table was heavy with rich dishes and Merlin suddenly found himself starving. Happenstance had been given a place of honour on a stool beside the king's chair. The two princesses fussed over him as he ate. Guinevere seemed to know everyone in the room. Although she sat beside Merlin, her head was constantly turned the other way to answer the greetings of her admirers.

"So you're Guinevere's student, are you?" asked Merlin's neighbour in a booming voice. The speaker had dark eyes and a rather squashed nose. He looked friendly, though.

"Yes," answered Merlin.

"Good to meet you," joined in the next man, who had a beard longer than King Stefan's. "You must have great potential to be chosen so young."

One by one the men introduced themselves: there was Lancel, and Fletcher, and another man named Sir Wynne. Merlin remembered where he had heard those names before – in stories told by travelling bards. They were the famous knights of King Stefan's court! They were brave and loyal protectors of the king. Merlin realised why Lancel's nose looked so much like a squashed tomato: it had been broken in a fight with his rival.

The knights quickly put Merlin at ease: they didn't once question the presence of a small eleven-year-old boy at their table. Instead, they made him gasp with tales of their adventures. He laughed at their jokes and then tried to awe them in return with stories of the magic he had witnessed in Eyrieland.

"I've heard about Guinevere's power," said Fletcher, "I heard that she cast a spell over a dragon that was close to killing the king-"

"It wasn't a dragon!" laughed Wynne, "It was a *bear*! A massive, wild creature. Guinevere took control of it and sent it off into the woods, away from the king. It was *this close*," he gestured, "To tearing him with its claws."

"Wow!" exclaimed Merlin. He wasn't entirely sure whether he believed all of the knights' stories, but they were nevertheless entertaining.

He was surprised to see that the sky outside had already faded to black; the meal had passed by in a happy blur. Guinevere called his name softly to attract his attention. Lancel, Fletcher and Wynne all turned towards her, too. She passed Merlin a small, silver medal. It felt heavy in his hand.

"King Stefan wanted to reward you," she explained. "He thought you would prefer to be given your prize quietly."

"My prize?" said Merlin, staring at the medal. He thought it must be worth more than everything else he and Murrow owned put together.

"Your reward for protecting your country from the sorcerer." Her eyes twinkled in the candlelight.

Lancel, Fletcher and Wynne cheered and clapped Merlin on the back.

"You've earned that, Merlin," said Wynne.

"I'm sure you'll make a terrific sorcerer," said Lancel, "With Guinevere to guide you. Just remember, magic isn't the key to everything. Sometimes you'll need to use this, too." He tapped Merlin playfully on the head.

Guinevere laughed, then left to join the guests dancing by the fire.

"Even if you decide not to follow Guinevere," said Wynne, "I'm sure we can expect great things from you."

Merlin felt his pale face flush. He held the medal up to the candle: it was marked with the king's seal. He was glad he'd slept on the way to the castle. After all the evening's excitement, Merlin wasn't sure he'd ever be able to sleep again.

Chapter Twenty-Two

Homeward Bound

Merlin, Guinevere and Happenstance stayed in the castle late into the night. When Guinevere at last took Merlin by the arm and led him out to the carriage, he was almost asleep on his feet. King Stefan's knights shook his hand and said they were certain that his path would cross with theirs again one day. The king himself carried Happenstance over to Merlin. He handed the dozy cat across and bid them both a fond farewell. Merlin wondered whether Guinevere really had saved the king's life.

The festivities in the castle carried on long after its guests of honour departed. A storm raged above the carriage as the blue horses raced along the road. Merlin looked outside the window, tired but triumphant after his long day. Guinevere sat with her head bowed. She looked asleep, but when Happenstance stretched and curled up on her lap she reached out to pat him. Merlin grasped his medal tightly in his hand. Not even the torrential rain, which splattered against the carriage, could dampen his spirits. He decided that even though he would miss home, even though he was afraid, and even though he'd miss Murrow every second, he had to go with Guinevere. He wanted to learn more about magic. His eyes had been opened up to a whole new world, a world of knights, quests and medals, and he wanted to be part of it. Happenstance meowed happily in his sleep.

The storm raged for hours. Merlin eventually fell asleep, curled up on the bench. A loud crack of thunder woke him up a while later. He had been in the middle of a strange dream in which a giant bird chased Murrow around the village. Guinevere was still silent, her face hidden behind curtains of red hair.

The sky had brightened up and the moon was full and bright. Merlin felt as though he was surrounded by magic; it was in the very air. His smile grew as he began to recognise where they were: he could see the outline of familiar hills. Best of all, in the distance he could hear the sound of the sea.

"We're almost home, Happenstance!" he whispered.

The blue servants that also sat in the carriage seemed to stare as he spoke. He still felt rather wary of them. He wondered if he'd ever have powers like Guinevere's. What happened if he wasn't able to become a sorcerer? How much did Guinevere already know about what was going to happen?

Guinevere stirred as the sun began to rise. The rain had stopped at last. Merlin smiled and said, "Morning, Guinevere!"

"Hello, Merlin. You should have got more sleep!"

Happenstance yawned on her lap.

"How close are we to the village?" asked Merlin. He was bouncing with excitement.

"Very close," answered Guinevere. "Your cottage is just over the next hill."

"Really?" said Merlin. He couldn't wait to tell Murrow all about his trip to Eyrieland.

"Yes," replied Guinevere. "I know you'll be eager to tell everyone about your adventures. Murrow will be thrilled to see your medal. I want you to remember, though, that my servants and I will be setting sail again tonight."

Merlin had almost forgotten that the carriage had been recently been ship-shaped.

"If you want to join me, please meet me in the woods tonight. We'll wait until the sun rises tomorrow. Bring Happenstance along, too, unless Murrow asks to keep him here. Make sure you ask your father what he thinks. If you decide to join me, I will show you how to earn magical powers of your own. I believe you could bring a lot of goodness to the world, Merlin. But you have to choose your own path. Either way, I'm grateful for your help in Eyrieland."

The carriage had slowed to a halt as she spoke.

"Walk over the hill and you'll see the cottage," instructed Guinevere, "Goodbye for now, Merlin."

She shook his hand: hers was very cold. Merlin whistled and Happenstance clambered up onto his shoulder.

"Goodbye, Guinevere. Thanks for everything!" smiled Merlin.

He climbed down out of the carriage. He raced up the hill (Happenstance's claws latched onto his shoulder in protest). When he cast a glance behind him, Guinevere, the carriage and the horses had already disappeared into the breeze.

Chapter Twenty-Three

Reunion

Merlin laughed out loud with joy to see his village again. The early morning air was cold but bright; the dewy grass soaked his feet as he ran. Happenstance jumped to the ground and bolted ahead. Merlin's thin legs propelled him forward as fast as he could after the cat. Already fishing boats were setting off from the harbour. Merlin hoped that Murrow hadn't decided to set off as early as those eager vessels.

The quiet cottages; the dark sea; the sights and smells of the village: Merlin didn't realise how much he'd missed his home. He had only been away for a short time, but a great deal had happened to him. Nothing in the village seemed to have changed at all. He even wondered whether he'd dreamed his whole adventure with Guinevere. Happenstance's hungry meow brought him out of his daydream. He raced to the cottage door and let the cat in first.

His father was snoring in front of the fire. He had wrapped himself up in all the blankets. At first Merlin couldn't tell which end was which, until Murrow let out an especially loud snore.

Merlin rushed over. He shook his father awake, calling "I'm home! I'm home!"

Murrow blinked at him for a few seconds before his face broke into a wide smile. "Merlin!" he cried, and sitting up, he hugged his son tightly.

Merlin couldn't imagine his father ever being lonely. Yet he understood then, perhaps for the first time, that he was the only family Murrow had left. He hugged his father tightly back. Happestance purred and rubbed himself around them.

"You're all the village has talked about, Merlin," said Murrow. "The other boys won't give you any peace now, you know!"

He stretched and lifted a pot of water onto the fire. "I bet you two are hungry!"

"Happenstance definitely is," said Merlin, with a laugh. "I've got something to show you!"

He held out the medal – it looked out of place in the cottage.

"Who gave you that, son?" asked Murrow. The sight of the medal drove the thought of breakfast from his mind.

"King Stefan," said Merlin. He blushed as he answered. He still wasn't sure that he'd really earned his reward.

"The KING?" exclaimed Murrow. "I thought Lady Guinevere was taking you to Eyrieland?"

"She did! We went there first, in the ship…"

"Wait until I get you two some breakfast, then tell me everything!" said Murrow. He ruffled his son's hair proudly.

Murrow and Merlin spoke until midday. They shared breakfast in front of the fire and took turns at admiring the medal. Murrow couldn't stop smiling: he had never expected such adventures to be possible. He clapped Merlin on the back when he heard how he had talked sense into the townsfolk in Eyrieland, and gave Happenstance a slightly mistrustful look when he learned that Guinevere had transformed him into a great hulking beast. He was pleased to hear that the knights had welcomed his son to their table with open arms. He would've almost expected them to be arrogant, since they were known and praised in every corner of the kingdom.

Merlin blushed again when his father said, "Lancel, Wynne and Fletcher, eh? I wonder if one day ballads will be sung about you?"

Happenstance slept happily on a pile of blankets. Watching his paws twitch, Merlin wondered if he dreamt of becoming ginormous again.

Murrow's relief to have his son delivered home safely was plain to see. He kept looking Merlin up and down, as if it had been years since he'd left the cottage.

"What did you learn about the Lady?" he asked, "We've been swapping theories about her in the village."

"Theories?" blinked Merlin. He didn't think he'd learned much about Guinevere at all. Only that her magic was terrific, but he had already told Murrow about that.

"Some people say we should be afraid of her. But I think they're just jealous of her interest in you."

Merlin didn't know what to say. He knew he would have been jealous if she'd swept into the village and granted one of the other boys the adventure of a lifetime.

"Do you know anything about the other sorcerers?" he asked his father.

"Not much – all we can do is guess. I don't think that sorcerer will risk another meeting with the Lady, though!"

Murrow looked at Merlin expectantly. Merlin steeled himself to tell Murrow what he'd decided to do. He was surprised to see that the father sat smiling in a knowing way.

"You're going to go with her, aren't you?"

"Yes…well, I think so. I want to," he said. He both did and didn't want to go: he hadn't quite had his fill of home yet.

"When will Guinevere come for you?" Murrow asked.

"I'm to meet her in the woods tonight. She invited Happenstance as well."

"Happenstance?" laughed Murrow. "I wonder why she's taken such a fancy to our lazy cat? Well, it'll definitely be quieter here without you both. But, Merlin," he said, more seriously, "This is too great a chance for you to turn down."

Merlin sat up and hugged his father. Murrow stroked his son's hair.

"You'll have to come and share your stories with the rest of the village before you go. You'll be the talk of the kingdom for years to come!"

Merlin smiled, "I will, but only if you keep the medal. Please, father – I want you to have it."

"Alright," answered Murrow, with a grin, "But only until you come to ask for it back."

Chapter Twenty-Four

Return to the Woods

The wind whistled around Merlin as he eased the cottage door shut. Murrow had wrapped him up in extra layers but his face was soon numb with the cold. After a long day in the village, Merlin had been close to falling asleep. As soon as darkness fell, however, he became awake again with anticipation.

Happenstance trotted on ahead. He was far too fat and fluffy to feel the cold. The sky was almost completely black as Merlin walked towards the woods. Thankfully, Happenstance looked back every now and then and Merlin was able to follow the lights of his eyes. The sea was in a raging temper; it stormed against the rocks. The cottage would be very damp by the morning. Merlin hoped Guinevere could calm the waves before they set sail.

Soon Merlin could see the floating lights in the distance. He sighed with relief. So much about Guinevere was too strange to be true – he still couldn't believe his luck. Happenstance waited for him by the edge of the woods. When Merlin caught up, the cat meowed and allowed Merlin to give him a quick comforting pat before prancing off again. The lights led them to the same place as before. Now he could no longer hear the roaring sea, but the rustling leaves were almost as loud.

Merlin followed Happenstance down into the clearing and grinned across at Guinevere. The red-haired sorcerer sat on a tree stump, with a fire of crackling leaves burning at her feet. Odd, twisting shapes rose in the smoke which billowed into the air.

Merlin counted all twelve of Guinevere's servants around the clearing. He called out hello to Guinevere, who waved across at him. She smiled, but her face, as Merlin drew closer, was somehow closed. Her face was thin and beautiful, but alien. It was nothing like the broad face of his father, about whom Merlin knew everything. For a second, he wanted nothing more than to walk away from Guinevere and go to sleep at home in his familiar bed.

Then the spell was broken. Guinevere waved away the billowing smoke and strode towards him. Happenstance rushed over to rub against her legs.

"I heard you've been the talk of the village today," she said.

"It's been weird! Everyone wanted to hear about your magic. They can't believe that I'll be going with you," said Merlin. Shivering, he moved closer to the fire.

"Can you?"

"Not really," said Merlin, with a laugh.

"I wouldn't have invited you if I didn't believe in you. But I need you to understand exactly what I expect of you before we set off."

Guinevere pointed to a tree stump behind Merlin, which definitely hadn't been there before. He sat down, facing Guinevere across the fire. Happenstance played with a stray leaf.

"You said before," said Merlin nervously, "That you don't know how long we'll be away for."

"You are quite right," Guinevere nodded. The wind blew the embers of the fire towards Merlin. It smelled of herbs and sweet flowers.

"You will have to earn your own magic, Merlin. I will teach you everything I know, but you have to prove yourself worthy first."

"But how?"

"Don't worry about that part yet. There will be several tests, but no two sorcerers are the same. You will not be put in any danger – and if you change your mind, I will bring you home."

Merlin nodded. Remembering the giant birds and biting wind, he wasn't sure he believed that the tests would be free of danger. But he did have Guinevere on his side.

"I promise you, Merlin, that if you ask, I will bring you home. If you or Happenstance face danger, I will do all I can to help you. If I am able to, all my knowledge of magic will be shared with you."

Guinevere's blue eyes stared straight into his. Merlin nodded again. After a second, he found his voice.

"Thank you…for all of this."

"You're welcome," said Guinevere. She looked almost surprised. Meanwhile, Happenstance's ears had pricked up at the mention of his name. "Now you need to promise too, Merlin."

"Alright," he said.

"Will you follow my instructions?"

He nodded.

"Will you tell me if you are homesick, or ill, or unhappy?"

Merlin nodded again.

"Do you understand that, whatever happens, you will not be the same boy when you return?"

"I understand," answered Merlin. He shared a smile with Guinevere as the wind howled between the trees.

Chapter Twenty-Five

Sailing Away

The next day was bright and warm. Everyone in the village had rushed to the harbour to see the sorcerer again. Even those who still suspected her of having dark powers were eager to take another look. When Murrow, Merlin and Happenstance (who was sitting snugly in Murrow's arms) arrived, they found a crowd gathered around the pier. Guinevere waited beside the grand ship. One of her servants came forward to take the sack of supplies from Merlin and carried it towards the ship. The villagers were still wary of the blue-skinned creatures – Merlin heard them sigh with relief when the rest followed onto the ship.

Merlin had been too sick with nerves to eat that morning. Murrow, meanwhile, had been unusually quiet. Only Happenstance seemed not to be much fussed about their upcoming adventure.

"Are you sure you don't want Happenstance to stay?" asked Merlin. He thought Happenstance looked far too comfortable in his father's arms.

"I need him to keep an eye on you," smiled Murrow.

He pulled his son into a hug, giving Merlin a mouthful of cat fur. An annoyed Happenstance squeezed out from between them to greet Guinevere.

Merlin breathed in the familiar scent of his father. He hoped he'd learn about a magical way of keeping in touch. Murrow patted him on the head.

"Good luck, Merlin. I'll take good care of that medal for you."

He hugged his son again. Merlin had never seen his father look so teary-eyed before. He couldn't find the words to answer, so he smiled sadly instead.

"Are you ready?" called Guinevere, walking to join them.

She held out her hand to Murrow. As they shook, the sorcerer whispered, "He'll be safe with me."

Murrow could only nod in reply. All the villagers watched them in silence.

Merlin said his final farewell to his father then followed Guinevere onto the ship. He waved goodbye to Murrow, the cottage and the village as he stood on deck. Guinevere joined him and stood in silence while he took a long look at his home.

The villagers started to shout messages of good luck as the ship began to move. Within moments, they had left the harbour far behind them. Guinevere's ship didn't need the wind to speed through the waves. At last Merlin turned away from the fading coastline. He crouched beside

Happenstance and called over to Guinevere, "Where is it that we're going?"

"To the place which holds the fountain of magical knowledge," answered Guinevere.

"And where's that?"

"Always so many questions," smiled Guinevere. "You'll see for yourself soon enough."

Smiling mysteriously, she disappeared into the cabin. Merlin grinned as he teased Happenstance with a piece of rope. He had so much to learn, and he couldn't wait to get started.

Merlin's adventures will continue…

Printed in Great Britain
by Amazon